This book belongs to

WHATEVER NEXT!

Jill Murphy

MACMILLAN CHILDREN'S BOOKS

First published 1983 by
MACMILLAN CHILDREN'S BOOKS
A division of Macmillan Publishers Limited
London and Basingstoke
Associated companies throughout the world

Picturemac edition published 1985
Reprinted 1986 (twice), 1987, 1988

British Library Cataloguing in Publication Data
Murphy, Jill
    Whatever next!
    I. Title
    823'.914[J]   PZ7
    ISBN 0-333-40438-6

Printed in Hong Kong

"Can I go to the moon?" asked Baby Bear.

"No you can't," said Mrs Bear.
"It's bathtime.
Anyway, you'd have to find a rocket first."

Baby Bear found a rocket
in the cupboard under the stairs.

He found a space-helmet
on the draining board in the kitchen,
and a pair of space-boots on the
mat by the front door.

He packed his teddy
and some food for the journey
and took off up the chimney . . .

. . . WHOOSH! Out into the night.

An owl flew past.
"That's a smart rocket," he said.
"Where are you off to?"
"The moon," said Baby Bear.
"Would you like to come too?"
"Yes please," said the owl.

An aeroplane roared out of the clouds.
Baby Bear waved and
some of the passengers waved back.

On and on they flew,
up and up, above the clouds,
past millions of stars till
at last they landed on the moon.

"There's nobody here," said Baby Bear.
"There are no trees," said the owl.
"It's a bit boring," said Baby Bear.
"Shall we have a picnic?"
"What a good idea," said the owl.

"We'd better go," said Baby Bear.
"My bath must be ready by now."
Off they went, down and down.
The owl got out and flew away.
"Goodbye," he said. "It was so nice
to meet you."

It rained and
the rain dripped through
Baby Bear's helmet.

Home went Baby Bear.
Back down the chimney
and on to the living room carpet
with a BUMP!

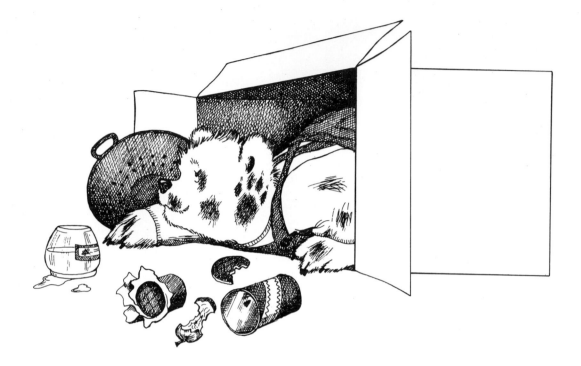

Mrs Bear came into the room.
"Look at the *state* of you!" she gasped
as she led him away to the bathroom.
"Why, you look as if you've been up the chimney."

"As a matter of fact," said Baby Bear,
"I *have* been up the chimney.
I found a rocket and went to
visit the moon."
Mrs Bear laughed.
"You and your stories," she said.
"Whatever next?"

Other Picturemacs you will enjoy

Anno's Counting Book   Mitsumasa Anno
A Walk in the Park   Anthony Browne
Creepy Castle   John Goodall
Jacko   John Goodall
The Midnight Adventures of Kelly, Dot and Esmeralda   John Goodall
Naughty Nancy the Bad Bridesmaid   John Goodall
Paddy's Evening Out   John Goodall
Shrewbettina's Birthday   John Goodall
The Surprise Picnic   John Goodall
Brown Bear in a Brown Chair   Irina Hale
Chocolate Mouse and Sugar Pig   Irina Hale
Donkey's Dreadful Day   Irina Hale
Maybe It's a Tiger   Kathleen Hersom/Niki Daly
Oh Lord!   Ron and Atie van der Meer
Peace at Last   Jill Murphy
"Ahhh!" Said Stork   Gerald Rose
Hector Protector   Maurice Sendak
The Surprise   George Shannon

For a complete list of Picturemac titles write to:

Publicity Department, Macmillan Children's Books,
4 Little Esscx Street, London WC2R 3LF